I Will Amaze You!

Written by Joe Elliot
Illustrated by Neil Sutherland, Blue-Zoo and Tony Trimmer

One day, e hid by a rock.

When he came out, he was all in black.
"Now I can do some tricks!" he said.

Soon, A came along.
"Hey!" said E. "Come and play!"

"Yay!" said A. "What shall we play?"

"I will do some tricks for you," said E.
"This will amaze you!"

g-a-m-e, game!
A green light went from **E** to **A**. It made
A say her name.

"Amazing!" said A. "We made a game!"

"Good trick, E!" said G.

"What can we do next?" said A.

c-a-k-e, cake!

"Mmm, we made a cake!" said M.

"Next trick!" said A.

c - a - v - e, cave!

"Cool! We made a cave!" said **C**.

A began to shake. "I am afraid!" she said.

"The cave is all grey!" said A. "There is no light!"
"Be brave!" said E.

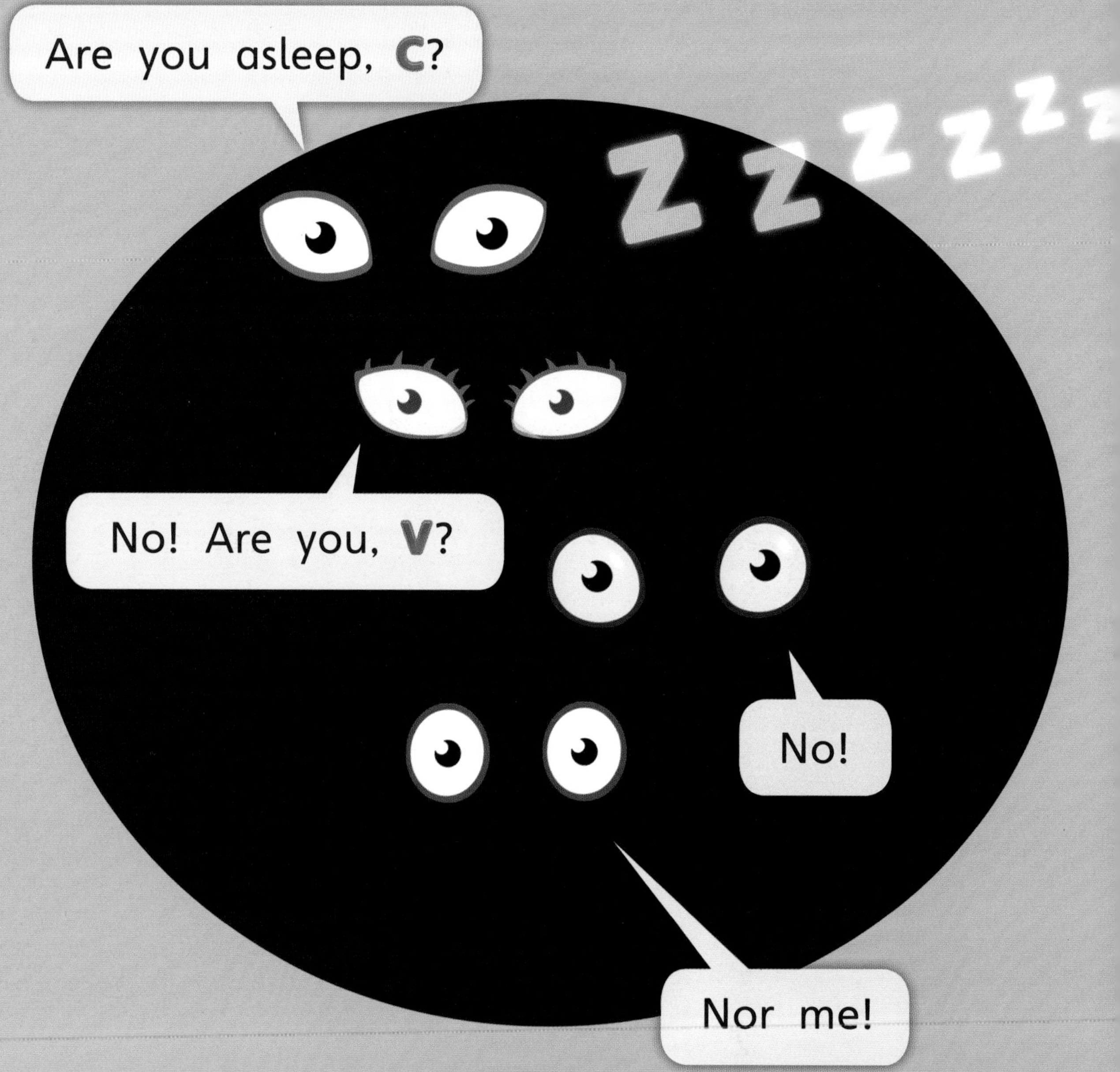
Are you asleep, C?
No! Are you, V?
No!
Nor me!

The monster came out of the cave.

It was Z, asleep on some zebras!
"Wake up, Z!" said C.

"Z!" said A. "You are not a monster!"
"No, just a letter that likes a nap!" said Z.

Z gave the reins a tug.

"Amazing!" said A. "A zebra bed!"

"That was the best trick of all!" said E.